REMARKABLE
CANADIANS

Nelly
Furtado

by Heather Kissock

Published by Weigl Educational Publishers Limited
6325 10 Street SE
Calgary, Alberta, Canada
T2H 2Z9

Website: www.weigl.com

Library and Archives Canada Cataloguing in Publication data available upon request.
Fax (403) 233-7769 for the attention of the Publishing Records department.

ISBN 978-1-55388-452-1 (hard cover)
ISBN 978-1-55388-453-8 (soft cover)

Printed in the United States of America
1 2 3 4 5 6 7 8 9 0   12 11 10 09 08

Editor: Heather C. Hudak
Design: Terry Paulhus

Photograph Credits
Weigl acknowledges Getty Images as the primary image supplier for this title.

Every reasonable effort has been made to trace ownership and to obtain
permission to reprint copyright material. The publishers would be pleased
to have any errors or omissions brought to their attention so that they may
be corrected in subsequent printings.

We gratefully acknowledge the financial support of the Government of Canada
through the Book Publishing Industry Development Program (BPIDP) for our
publishing activities.

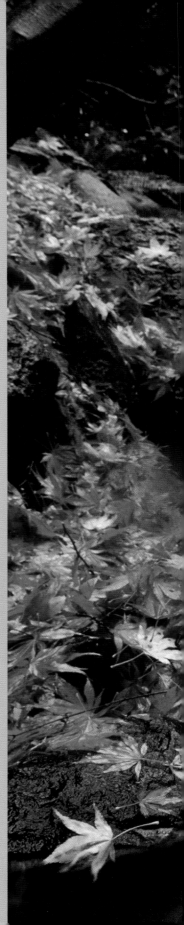

Contents

Who Is Nelly Furtado?

Singer-songwriter Nelly Furtado is one of Canada's best-known faces. With songs such as *Like a Bird* and *Say it Right*, she has gained worldwide success. Nelly's music is known for its unique sound. She stretches musical boundaries by combining many forms of music, from pop to rap to Portuguese folk music. As a result, Nelly's music appeals to a large number of people. This has led to much praise and many awards, including Canadian Juno Awards, American Grammy Awards, and Brit Awards from Great Britain.

"I feel like if you can get down with any style of music, you can get down with any style of person. So it's fun for me—I get to expose my fans to different vibes and they, in turn, open their minds too."

Growing Up

Nelly Kim Furtado was born on December 2, 1978, in Victoria, British Columbia. Nelly is a first generation Canadian. Her parents came from Portugal. They **immigrated** to Canada in the 1960s. Her father, António, was a landscaper, while her mother, Maria, worked as a housekeeper. Nelly is the youngest of three children. She has both an older sister and an older brother.

Throughout Nelly's childhood, the Furtado family had a great love of music. Nelly's mother sang in a church choir. Her father had a huge record collection that included many different types of music. He was a fan of a Portuguese folk music. Both of Nelly's parents loved to sing and urged their children to share their love of music. Nelly has credited her musical success to her parents and the love of music they shared with her.

🍁 The Empress Hotel, located along Victoria's Inner Harbour, is one of the city's main highlights.

British Columbia Tidbits

ANIMAL
Spirit Bear

FLOWER
Pacific Dogwood

BIRD
Stellar's Jay

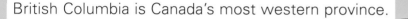

British Columbia is Canada's most western province.

Mountains cover about 75 percent of British Columbia. Mountain ranges in the province include the Coast Mountains, the Columbia Mountains, and the Rocky Mountains.

Vancouver is the largest city in British Columbia. About two million people live in the city and its surrounding communities.

British Columbia was the sixth province to join **Confederation**. It became part of Canada on July 20, 1871.

Victoria is the capital city of British Columbia. It is located on the southern tip of Vancouver Island.

Nelly grew up on an island that was separated from the rest of the country. How do you think this may have affected Nelly when she was growing up? How might it have influenced her music?

Practice Makes Perfect

Music was an important part of Nelly's home life. By the time she was four years old, Nelly could play the ukelele and sing songs in both English and Portuguese. She even performed duets with her mother in church. When she reached school age, Nelly found even more chances to explore and develop her musical talents.

Nelly took part in the school's music programs. She learned to play trombone. This led to her becoming a member of several groups, including a jazz band, the school's concert band, and a Portuguese marching band. Nelly's vocal talents were noticed as well, and she was often cast in school musicals.

🌷 Nelly taught herself to play guitar. The first song she learned to play was *Wonderwall* by Oasis.

By the time she graduated from high school, Nelly could play guitar and was beginning to write songs. After high school, Nelly moved to Toronto, Ontario, where she lived with her sister. She began to spend time with people in Toronto's music industry. Toronto had an active hip-hop scene, and Nelly soon formed a **trip-hop** group called Nelstar with another musician. By the end of the year, the group broke up, and Nelly decided to move back to Victoria.

QUICK FACTS

- When she was eight years old, Nelly was given a tape recorder and microphone as a gift. She used the tape recorder to record music that interested her. She also used the machine to practise her singing.

- Along with her parents, Nelly considers her brother to be a strong influence in her life. He introduced her to rock bands such as Radiohead, Oasis, and U2.

- While in Toronto, Nelly performed back-up vocals on an **album** by hip-hop group Plains of Fascination.

Many music festivals, events, and companies, such as the Canadian Opera Company and the Toronto Symphony Orchestra, are found in Toronto.

Key Events

Before Nelly returned to Victoria, she performed one last time in Toronto. The event was an **urban** talent show. A man named Gerald Eaton was in the audience during Nelly's show. He was the lead singer of a Canadian band called The Philosopher Kings. Gerald enjoyed Nelly's performance. After the show, he offered to help Nelly with her music career. Together with Brian West, another member of The Philosopher Kings, Nelly and Gerald began writing songs for a **demo** record.

After recording the demo, Nelly returned to Victoria. There, she attended Camosun College as a creative writing student. Brian and Gerald asked Nelly to return to Toronto to write and record more songs. She finally agreed, and they began working together again.

When the demo was finished, they sent it to DreamWorks Records. Dreamworks signed Nelly to a **recording contract**, and she began working on her first album, "Whoa Nelly!" Gerald and Brian **produced** the album.

The first **single** from the album was *Like a Bird*. Very quickly, the song became popular, and millions of copies were sold. Nelly began a tour, giving performances across North America.

🍁 Gerald Eaton also performs under the name Jarvis Church.

Thoughts from Nelly

From a young age, Nelly dreamed of being a performer. Here are some of the things she has said about her music and her life.

Nelly explains her approach to using different styles of music in her work.

"I look at music with a very open mind and really wide lens. When you don't have any boundaries, you're limitless, you can do anything because you have no **bias**."

Like many people, Nelly admits to being caught up with pop culture.

"I love it. I can't help it—I love awards shows, magazines, movies. I'm totally star-struck."

Nelly wants to be a role model for children with Portuguese backgrounds.

"I'd never see any Portuguese people on TV, and that really struck a major chord with me. And so I was like 'One day I'm gonna be on TV, and Portuguese kids are gonna see me on TV and they're gonna feel proud, they're gonna feel right.'"

Nelly explains how living in Toronto has influenced her.

"...Toronto is the most multicultural city in the entire world. ...you can be anything you want in Toronto."

Nelly describes how she has always been a free spirit.

"I was always that kid in high school who would show up with different outfits every day. One day, preppy. One day, skater. One day, hippie. It was always in my nature to try everything. That's what my career will always be like. I'm always going to be changing."

Nelly talks about her relationship with Gerald Eaton and Brian West.

"...when I work with them, my music comes together really quickly, very effortlessly. And it's fun which, above all, music should be. If you're not having fun there's no point."

What Is a Singer-Songwriter?

Nelly Furtado is a singer-songwriter. This means that she writes most of the songs that she sings. Being a singer-songwriter allows Nelly to add her personal touch to her music. She can express events and emotions the way she sees and feels them, and share these thoughts with her audience.

Most singer-songwriters have a solid knowledge of how to make music. They understand that music can be written in different keys to match their **vocal range** and to set a mood. They know how notes can be put together to create **chords** and **harmonies**. Using these skills, singer-songwriters have the freedom to express themselves.

🍁 Nelly started singing into a tape recorder at age 8 and writing rhymes at 14.

Singer-Songwriters 101

Feist (1976–)

Music Alternative
Achievements After years of working as an **indie** rock artist, Feist became known around the world with the release of her 2007 album, The Reminder. The album received four Grammy **nominations** and won several Juno awards. In 2002, Feist joined the indie rock group Broken Social Scene. The group won two Junos in 2003. After the release of her solo album, Let It Die, in 2004, Feist was awarded Junos for Best New Artist and Best Alternative Rock Album.

Avril Lavigne (1984–)

Music Pop/rock
Achievements In 2002, Avril Lavigne's first album, Let Go, was released. It quickly became a hit, selling almost 14 million copies less than six months after its release. As a result of this success, Avril has been awarded an MTV Video Music Award, seven Juno awards, and several Grammy nominations. Her music continues to top music charts. In 2007, Avril's single, *Girlfriend*, **debuted** on the Billboard Hot 100 at number five.

Chantal Kreviazuk (1973–)

Music Adult **Contemporary**/Pop
Achievements Known for writing lyrics that express deep feelings, Chantal Kreviazuk has had top 40 hits both in Canada and the United States. Both her first album, Under These Rocks and Stones, and her second album, Colour Moving and Still, have sold millions of copies. Chantal won two Juno awards for Colour Moving and Still.

Sam Roberts (1974–)

Music Rock
Achievements Sam Robert is known as a thoughtful **lyricist** who can put a rock song together well. In 2003, Sam released his first album. He was nominated for two Juno awards and several MuchMusic Video Awards. The next year, Sam's album, We Were Born in a Flame, won Junos for Album of the Year and Rock Album of the Year. That same year, Sam won the Juno for Artist of the Year. In 2007, he won the Juno for Video of the Year.

Juno Awards

Canada's Juno Awards celebrate excellence in Canadian music. They have been awarded to musicians, producers, and music technicians since the early 1970s. At a ceremony held every year, awards are given to recording artists from a range of musical styles, including rock, jazz, country, and classical. The ceremony is held in a different Canadian city each year.

Influences

Nelly has always credited her musical success to her parents. They introduced her to many musical styles when she was young and encouraged her to sing. However, Nelly has also said that her parents gave her a strong work **ethic** as well. They understood that people had to work hard if they wanted to be successful. They passed this belief on to Nelly, who used it to reach her goal of being a performer.

Living in a music-loving home exposed Nelly to a range of musical styles. These all helped influence her as a performer. Nelly's earliest musical experiences were with Portuguese folk music. This music has stayed with Nelly throughout her life, and she often includes a Portuguese song on her albums. *Fado*, a type of Portuguese music, is very similar to rap music. Nelly's understanding of fado helps her feel comfortable performing rap in her songs.

🍁 Fado, folk music, and traditional dance are important parts of Portuguese culture today.

As Nelly grew older, she heard the musical styles of other artists. Some of the people she listened to included Jeff Buckley, Janet Jackson, Mary J. Blige, and Mariah Carey. By listening to these people, Nelly was able to mix different sounds into her music.

Nelly's move to Toronto was a turning point in her life. Toronto is a multicultural city. Being there allowed Nelly to hear even more types of music. By trying to use different music styles in her own songs, Nelly continued to grow as an artist.

JEFF BUCKLEY

Jeff Buckley was one of the most gifted musicians of the 1990s. Like Nelly, he tried many musical styles, ranging from blues to punk. Jeff's music earned the respect of critics, other artists, and the public. His career was strong when he drowned in a Tennessee river, in 1997. Many of today's top performers, including Coldplay, John Legend, and Nelly Furtado, say Jeff was an important musical influence.

🍁 Nelly Furtado has said that Jeff Buckley's album Grace changed her life and influenced her singing, writing, and performing.

When Nelly was growing up, she sometimes felt different because of her Portuguese background. Beyond family and friends, Nelly had very few Portuguese role models. This was because Portuguese culture was rarely portrayed on television or in the movies. Aside from her family, Nelly had no one to use as an example for reaching her goals.

Instead of letting this make her upset, Nelly decided to use her musical talents to become a role model for other Portuguese children. She focussed her energy on her music. Over time, Nelly became the type of role model she had wished for in her youth.

NELLY FURTADO

Nelly has become a role model for Portuguese children around the world.

It was these roots that Nelly wanted to explore on her second album, "Folklore." Her first album sold many copies, but Nelly wanted to try a different style on her second album. She moved away from the bouncy pop sounds of her first album and wrote songs about her feelings and events in her own life. When the album was released, it did not sell as well as her first album.

When it was time for Nelly to record her third album, she went in a different direction once again. This time, she used a mix of urban and hip hop sounds. To help her create this new sound, Nelly invited people such as singer Justin Timberlake and producer Timbaland to work on the album. The result was Nelly's best-selling album, "Loose."

"Loose" sold more than 218,000 copies in its first week of sales.

Achievements and Successes

Nelly's music has attracted fans all over the world. Her music also has drawn attention from people in the music industry. This has led to Nelly receiving many nominations and awards for her work.

For her first album, "Whoa, Nelly!", Nelly received four Grammy nominations. She won for Best Female Pop Vocal Performance on the single, *Like a Bird*. This single reached number one in Canada and was a top 10 hit in the United States and Europe. "Whoa, Nelly!" has sold more than five million copies worldwide.

In total, Nelly has received seven Grammy nominations.

Nelly's third album, "Loose," was even more successful. For it, Nelly earned nominations at the Grammy Awards, the Brit Awards, the Junos, and the MTV Europe Awards. She received the Brit Award for International Female Solo Artist and the MTV Europe Music Award for Album of the Year. At Canada's Junos, Nelly won in every category for which she was nominated. She has won five Junos in total.

Nelly continues to push herself in new directions. She has tried acting and has been on television series such as *CSI: NY*. As well, Nelly became mother, after giving birth to a daughter named Nevis in 2003.

❧ The song *Give It to Me*, featuring Nelly Furtado, Justin Timberlake, and Timbaland, reached number one on the *Billboard Hot 100* chart.

NELLY'S CHARITY WORK

Nelly shows her concern for the world by working for different causes and charities. In 2006, she performed at a concert in South Africa that promoted AIDS awareness. She also hosted a program about AIDS for MTV. In Toronto, Nelly is one of the sponsors for the Dovercourt Boys and Girls Club. The club provides young people a chance to learn and have fun in a safe environment. In British Columbia, Nelly supports The Land Conservancy. This is an organization that works to preserve natural sites in the province.

Write a Biography

A person's life story can be the subject of a book. This kind of book is called a biography. Biographies describe the lives of remarkable people, such as those who have achieved great success or have done important things to help others. These people may be alive today, or they may have lived many years ago. Reading a biography can help you learn more about a remarkable person.

At school, you might be asked to write a biography. First, decide who you want to write about. You can choose a singer-songwriter such as Nelly Furtado, or any other person you find interesting. Then, find out if your library has any books about this person. Learn as much as you can about him or her. Write down the key events in this person's life. What was this person's childhood like? What has he or she accomplished? What are his or her goals? What makes this person special or unusual?

A concept web is a useful research tool. Read the questions in the following concept web. Answer the questions in your notebook. Your answers will help you write your biography review.

- Where does this individual currently reside?
- Does he or she have a family?

- What did you learn from the books you read in your research?
- Would you suggest these books to others?
- Was anything missing from these books?

- Where and when was this person born?
- Describe his or her parents, siblings, and friends.
- Did this person grow up in unusual circumstances?

Your Opinion

Adulthood

Childhood

WRITING A BIOGRAPHY

Main Accomplishments

Help and Obstacles

Work and Preparation

- What is this person's life's work?
- Has he or she received awards or recognition for accomplishments?
- How have this person's accomplishments served others?

- What was this person's education?
- What was his or her work experience?
- How does this person work; what is or was the process he or she uses or used?

- Did this individual have a positive attitude?
- Did he or she receive help from others?
- Did this person have a mentor?
- Did this person face any hardships?
- If so, how were the hardships overcome?

Timeline

YEAR	NELLY FURTADO	WORLD EVENTS
1978	Nelly Kim Furtado is born on December 2.	The Walkman, the first portable stereo, is introduced.
1996	Nelly moves to Toronto.	Janet Jackson signs an $80 million deal with Virgin Records, becoming the highest paid musician in history.
1997	Nelly performs at a talent show and meets Gerald Eaton of the Philosopher Kings.	Canadian Sarah McLachlan wins the Grammy for Best Female Pop Vocal Performance.
1999	Nelly signs a record deal with DreamWorks Records.	Christina Aguilera releases her first album. The first single *Genie in a Bottle* reaches number one on the charts.
2000	Nelly's first album, "Whoa Nelly!," is released.	Britney Spears releases her second album. It debuts at number one, the highest debut ever for a female recording artist.
2003	Nelly's second album, "Folklore," is released. She gives birth to daughter Nevis.	Apple introduces iTunes, an Internet music store.
2006	Nelly releases her third album, "Loose."	The one-billionth song is downloaded on iTunes. The song is *Speed of Sound* by Coldplay.

Further Research

How can I find out more about Nelly Furtado?

Most libraries have computers that connect to a database that contains information on books and articles about different subjects. You can input a key word and find material on that person, place, or thing you want to learn more about. The computer will provide you with a list of books in the library that contain information on the subject you searched for. Non-fiction books are arranged numerically, using their call number. Fiction books are organized alphabetically by the author's last name.

Websites

To learn more about Nelly, visit her official website at www.nellyfurtado.com

To find out more about the Juno Awards, go to www.junoawards.ca

Words to Know

album: a group of songs placed on a CD

bias: to have strong feelings or opinions about something

chords: the playing of three or more musical notes together

Confederation: the creation of Canada as a nation in 1867

contemporary: modern

debuted: made a first appearance

demo: a recorded sample of songs

ethic: a moral value

harmonies: notes that complement each other when played together

immigrated: came to another place

indie: not contracted to a record company

lyricist: someone who writes a song's words

nominations: named as a candidate for an award

produced: arranged for an album to be made and steered the creative people

recording contract: a written agreement to make albums for a music company

single: a song sent out for radio stations to play

trip hop: a form of music that combines hip hop with melodic sounds

urban: street music

vocal range: the spread of notes from low to high that someone can sing

Index